# THE
# APRIL
# RABBITS

## by David Cleveland
## Illustrations by Nurit Karlin

## SCHOLASTIC INC.
New York  Toronto  London  Auckland  Sydney

To Charlotte
—D.C.

To Ada and Alma
—N.K.

ISBN 0-590-42369-X

Text copyright © 1978 by David J. Cleveland. Illustrations copyright © 1978 by Nurit Karlin. All rights reserved. This edition is published by Scholastic Inc., 730 Broadway, New York, NY 10003, by arrangement with Coward, McCann & Geoghegan, Inc.

12 11 10 9 8 7 6 5 4                    0 1 2 3/9

Printed in the U.S.A.                    08

On the first day of April the sun was shining, birds were chirping, and a rabbit was nibbling on a bush as Robert went off to school.

On the second day of April Robert scared two rabbits
across the road as he walked to his tuba lesson.

On the third day of April he thought for a minute that he saw three rabbits in skirts tap-dancing on the windowsill.

On the fourth day of April he felt there was something
rabbity about the living room as he watched TV.

On the fifth of April Robert found five half-eaten carrots at the very bottom of his toy box.

While fishing on the sixth, he saw six rabbits paddle by in a canoe.

On the seventh day of April there were seven rabbits
singing with a cat on the garage roof.

Eight rabbits left their bikes in the driveway on the eighth.

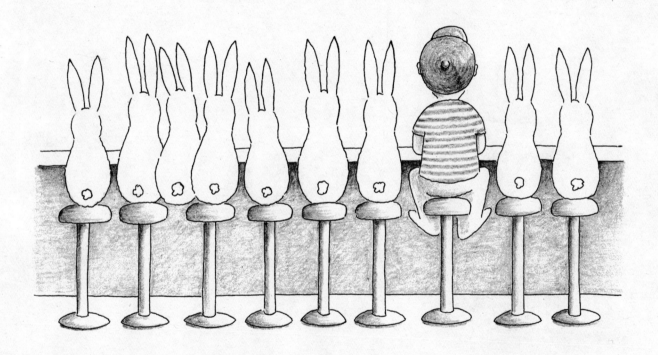

All nine seats at the soda fountain were taken by rabbits
on the ninth, but they made room for Robert.

On the tenth Robert noticed ten funny holes in the lawn as
he took out the garbage for his mother.

On the eleventh of April
eleven rabbits on skateboards
whizzed down Elm Street.

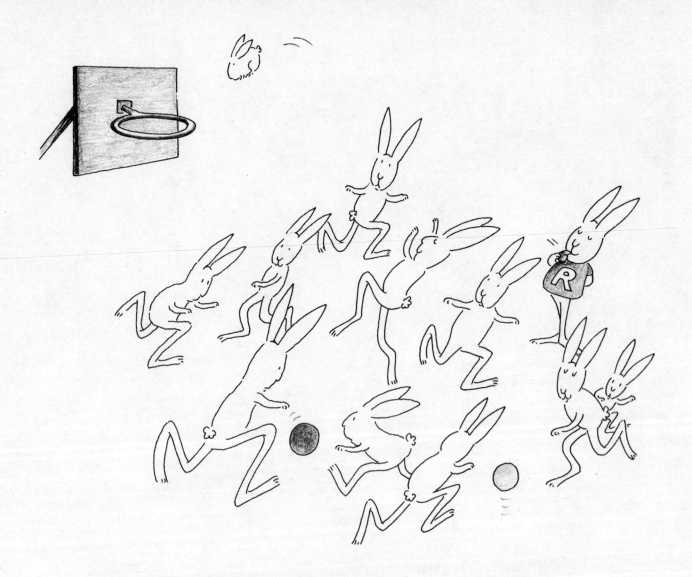

There were twelve rabbits playing basketball at the playground on the twelfth.

On the thirteenth there were thirteen rabbits in the supermarket.

There were fourteen rabbits at the clothesline on April fourteenth.

On the fifteenth Robert's mother took him to the eye doctor because she thought he was seeing things. There were fifteen patients ahead of him.

On the sixteenth Robert found sixteen rabbits making
double-decker peanut butter and radish sandwiches
in the kitchen.

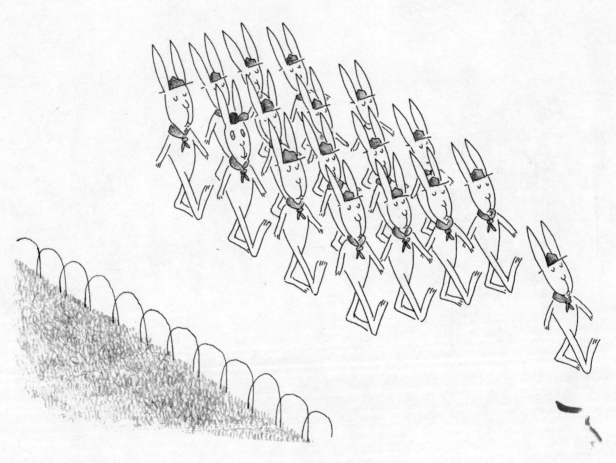

Seventeen rabbits in Scout uniforms marched by in a line
on the seventeenth.

On the eighteenth Robert thought he spotted a flock of
eighteen rabbits fly over his head and land in a nearby tree.

On the nineteenth of April nineteen tiny rabbits jumped
out of a bag of pretzels and ran in all directions.

On the twentieth of April twenty rabbits in funny hats gave
a birthday party in the dining room.

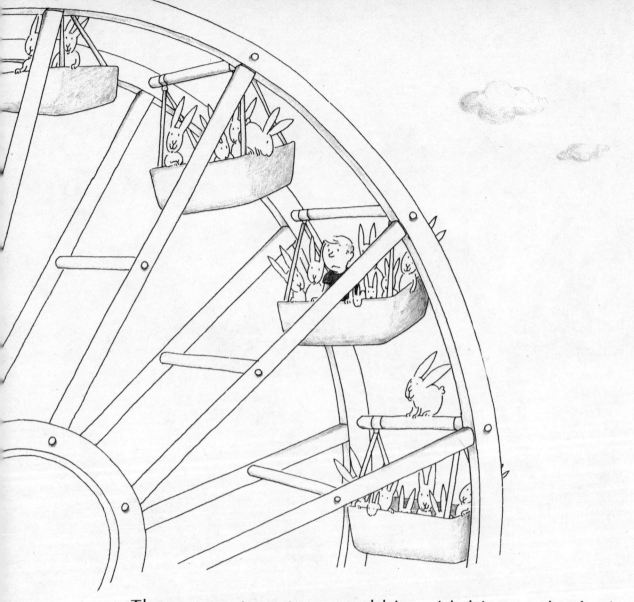

There were twenty-one rabbits with him on the ferris wheel
at the amusement park on the twenty-first.

On the twenty-second, twenty-two crazy rabbits tried on all his clothes, including his favorite baseball cap.

Robert found twenty-three rabbits taking a nap in his bedroom on the twenty-third.

The next day a busload of twenty-four rabbits
stopped next to him at the corner and all the passengers
made faces at him through the windows.

Twenty-five rabbits all took out books ahead of him
at the library on the twenty-fifth, but he still got the book
he wanted.

On the twenty-sixth, twenty-six rabbits took a bath in his tub and used up all the bubble bath.

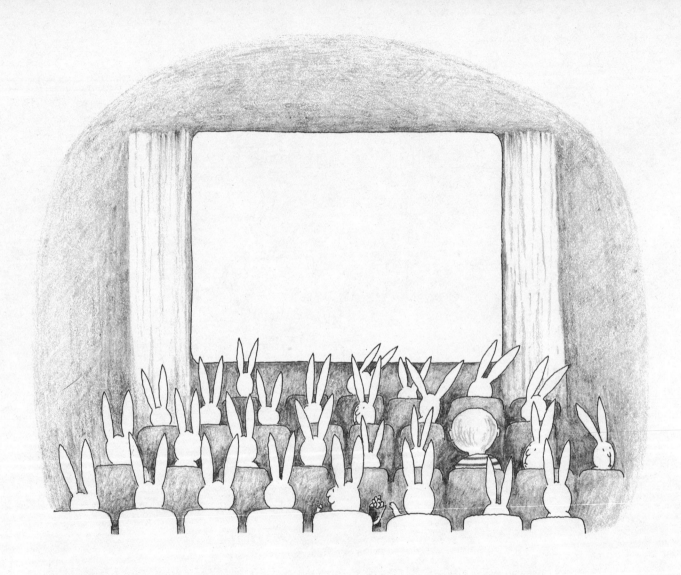

In the movies on the twenty-seventh, Robert sat in the
midst of twenty-seven rabbits crunching popcorn.

On the twenty-eighth of April twenty-eight rabbits camped out all night in the backyard, telling stories and roasting a giant head of lettuce on the campfire.

On the twenty-ninth day of April twenty-nine rabbits with suitcases tiptoed down the driveway and out of sight.

On the last day of April Robert watched very carefully all day long, but he didn't see a single rabbit.

Anywhere.

That night, a hippopotamus followed him home.